A Little Bit Lucky

Ready, Freddy!

#1: Tooth Trouble
#2: The King of Show-and-Tell
#3: Homework Hassles
#4: Don't Sit on My Lunch!
#5: Talent Show Scaredy-Pants
#6: Help! A Vampire's Coming!
#7: Yikes! Bikes!
#8: Halloween Fraidy-Cat
#9: Shark Tooth Tale
#10: Super-Secret Valentine
#11: The Pumpkin Elf Mystery
#12: Stop That Hamster!
#13: The One Hundredth Day of School!
#14: Camping Catastrophe!
#15: Thanksgiving Turkey Trouble
#16: Ready, Set, Snow!
#17: Firehouse Fun!
#18: The Perfect Present
#19: The Penguin Problem
#20: Apple Orchard Race
#21: Going Batty
#22: Science Fair Flop
#23: A Very Crazy Christmas
#24: Shark Attack!
#25: Save the Earth!
#26: The Giant Swing
#27: The Reading Race

2nd Grade

#1: Second Grade Rules!
#2: Snow Day Dare
#3: Secret Santa Surprise
#4: Best Prank Ever
#5: Haunted Hayride
#6: Gingerbread Jitters
#7: A Little Bit Lucky

Ready, Freddy!

A Little Bit Lucky

by ABBY KLEIN

illustrated by
JOHN McKINLEY

Scholastic Inc.

To Lucas and Leila:
Two of the coolest kids I know!
Here's hoping you always have a little bit of luck!
Love,
A.K.

ISBN 978-0-545-93176-2

10 9 8 7 6 5 4 3 19 20 21

Printed in the U.S.A. 40

First printing 2017

Book design by Mary Claire Cruz

CHAPTERS

I have a problem.

A really, really big problem.

The Second Grade Spelling Bee is coming up, and I'm not going to spell any words right because I've lost my lucky shark's tooth!

Let me tell you about it.

CHAPTER 1

Lucky Duck

RINNNGGG! RINNNGGG! My alarm clock screamed in my ear. I smacked the snooze button and covered my head with my pillow.

I don't want to get up, I thought to myself. *Just let me sleep ten more minutes.*

I closed my eyes again and was just drifting off to sleep when my sister, Suzie, barged into my room and yelled in my ear, "Get up, Sharkbreath!"

I swatted my hand in her direction. "Go away!" I shouted. "Leave me alone!"

"You have to be downstairs for breakfast in

five minutes," said Suzie, "or you're going to be late for the bus."

"You're not my mother!" I growled. Then I picked up my pillow and threw it at her.

Suzie jumped out of the way, and the pillow landed with a thud on the floor. "Missed me!" she said, smiling.

"I'll get up when I want to," I said, pulling the covers over my head. "Now get out!"

Suzie didn't move. I could still hear her breathing.

"Did you not hear me? I said get out!"

Suzie picked up the pillow, whacked me on the head, and marched out of the room.

"You're so annoying!" I yelled after her.

I sat up slowly, stretched my arms up high, and yawned. I walked over to my dresser, pulled out my favorite shark shirt, and put it on.

I wandered into the bathroom and brushed my teeth with my eyes half closed, as toothpaste dribbled down my chin.

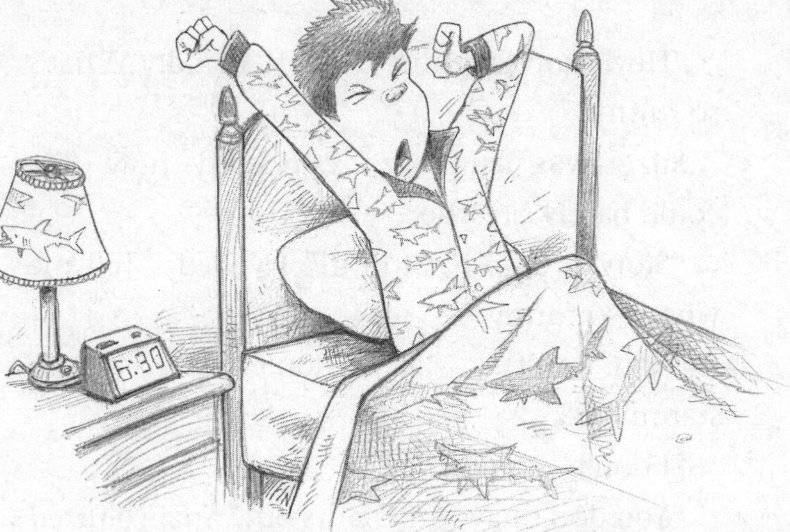

I rinsed out my mouth and slowly made my way downstairs. I practically crawled into the kitchen.

"Wow! I don't think a snail could move any slower," said my dad.

"You look like you're sleepwalking," said my mom.

I yawned again. "I think I might be sleepwalking," I said.

All of a sudden, Suzie pointed at me and started to laugh. "HA! HA! HA! HA! HA!"

"Hey! Stop laughing at me!" I said. "What's so funny?"

Suzie was laughing hysterically now. She could barely breathe.

"Stop it! Stop it! Stop it!" I yelled. "Tell me what's so funny!"

"You don't . . . you don't . . . ," Suzie stammered.

"I don't . . . what?"

"You don't have any pants on!" Suzie blurted out.

I slowly looked down at my legs. I had on my undies, but no pants. My legs were bare.

"You must have been half asleep when you got dressed this morning," said my mom.

"You'd better go put on some pants," said my dad. "I don't think you want to go to school dressed like that!"

"I think you *should* go in just your underwear," said Suzie. "That would be hilarious!"

"Oh yeah, really funny," I said.

"Well, you'd better hurry up, Freddy," said my mom. "You don't have a lot of time before the bus comes, and you still haven't eaten your breakfast."

I jogged out of the kitchen and ran upstairs to get a pair of pants. I looked around my room for my jeans. I found them on the floor in the corner and put them on. Then I slid down the banister, raced into the kitchen, and skidded into my seat at the table.

"Much better," said my mom.

"Good thing I have my pants on," I said, smiling.

"I'll say," said my dad. "I don't think you want to go to school naked. That could be quite embarrassing!"

"No," I said, laughing. "I mean it's a good thing I have my pants on because I always keep my lucky shark's tooth in my pocket. If I didn't have my pants on, I wouldn't have my lucky shark's tooth."

"I can't believe you think that dumb shark's tooth is lucky," said Suzie.

"First of all, it's not dumb. And second of all, it *is* lucky," I said, patting my pocket.

"Oh really?" said Suzie. "I don't believe it."

"It is!" I said. "I'll show you."

"You're going to show me?" said Suzie. "How are you going to show me?"

"Just watch," I said. I turned to my mom. "Can I please have the Tooty Fruity O's for breakfast?"

"Sure, honey," said my mom, and she went to get the Tooty Fruity O's out of the cupboard.

"I thought you were going to show me," said Suzie.

"I am. Just wait a minute," I said.

My mom came back with the cereal. "Here you go, honey."

I picked up the box and shoved it in Suzie's face. "Do you see there is a secret Commander Upchuck surprise in this box? You can get

Commander Upchuck, his dog Cookie, or his spaceship."

"Yeah," said Suzie. "So what?"

"So I know which surprise I'm going to get."

"No, you don't!"

"Yes, I do!"

"Do not!"

"Do too!"

"Fine," said Suzie. "Which surprise are you going to get?"

"The spaceship."

"How can you be so sure?"

"Because my lucky shark's tooth always brings me good luck. All I have to do is rub it before I reach my hand into the cereal box."

"I still don't believe it," said Suzie.

"Then watch and be amazed," I said. I stuck my hand in my pocket and rubbed my lucky shark's tooth. Then I reached into the cereal box and felt around with my hand until I found the prize.

"Hurry up already!" said Suzie. "We haven't got all morning."

"Hold on to your pants!" I said.

"At least I didn't forget to put mine on this morning," said Suzie.

I started to slowly pull the prize out of the box.

Suzie glared at me and tapped her fingers on the table.

"Are you ready?" I asked Suzie.

"Ready, Freddy. Pull it out already!"

"TA-DA!" I announced as I yanked the prize free.

Suzie stared at the prize in my hand. Her eyes got big and wide.

"It's the spaceship!" I shouted, waving the toy in the air. "The one I wanted."

"WOW!" said Suzie. "That *is* a lucky shark's tooth."

"Told you so," I said, smiling. "It always brings me good luck."

CHAPTER 2

Exciting News

Even though I was a bit late finishing my breakfast, the bus also happened to be a little late, so I didn't miss it. That was lucky! I patted the shark's tooth in my pocket.

When we arrived at school, Robbie, Josh, and I walked down the hall together. My best friend Robbie wasn't in my class this year, so every morning we made plans to meet up at recess.

"What do you guys want to do today at recess?" Robbie asked.

"Let's play tag!" I suggested. "We haven't played that in a while."

"Nah, I don't feel like that today," said Josh.

"Besides," said Robbie. "Max always plays tag lately, and he pushes everyone when he tags them. Yesterday, I saw him push Dean so hard, Dean went flying to the ground."

"Max really needs to learn how to play by the rules," said Josh. "He's always hurting other kids."

We nodded. The biggest bully in the whole second grade never played by the rules.

"I know!" said Josh. "We could play soccer."

"I do love to play soccer, but we've been doing that a lot lately. I'm getting kind of tired of it," I said.

"I've got it!" said Robbie. "Let's look for worms! It rained last night, so we should be able to find a lot of them."

"That's a great idea!" I said.

"Yeah," Josh agreed. "I love doing that. We can ask Jessie if she wants to go worm hunting, too."

We all high-fived each other. Then the bell rang for school to start.

"We'd better get going," I said. "We don't want to be late."

"See you guys at recess!" Robbie yelled as he disappeared down the hall.

"Yeah, meet you by the big tree," Josh and I called back.

We walked into our classroom and started to put our stuff away.

"Good morning, boys," said our teacher, Miss Clark. "How are you this morning?"

"Good," said Josh.

"Great!" I said, smiling.

"I'm glad to hear that, Freddy," said Miss Clark. "What has made your morning so great?"

I pulled the Commander Upchuck spaceship out of my backpack and held it up for her to see. "This!" I said with a big grin on my face.

"What is that?" asked Miss Clark.

"It's a Commander Upchuck spaceship. I found it in my Tooty Fruity O's this morning."

Max whipped his head around. "No way!" he shouted. Then he came running over and grabbed it out of my hands. "I've been wanting this for so long. How did you get this? You are soooooo lucky!"

"Max, you need to give that back to Freddy. You can't just grab something out of someone's hands like that," said Miss Clark.

Max ignored her and kept turning the spaceship over in his hands and staring at it. "This is so cool."

"Max, did you hear me?" said Miss Clark, tapping him on the shoulder. "That belongs to Freddy. Please give it back to him."

Max looked at Miss Clark, and he looked at me.

"Now, Max," Miss Clark said a little bit louder.

Max sighed, and then he handed the spaceship back to me.

"Thank you," said Miss Clark. "Now go finish putting your things away."

Max walked back over to the cubbies, but Chloe had arrived and was hanging up her coat. Instead of waiting for her to finish, Max shoved her out of the way.

Chloe lost her balance, dropped her lunch box, and accidentally sat down right on top of it. "Oh no! Oh no, you big bully! Look what you made me do!" she cried.

Max did not even turn around.

"This is my brand-new pink ballerina lunch

box, and now it's smushed!" she wailed. "My nana just gave it to me yesterday!"

Miss Clark came running over. "Here, Chloe," she said, extending her hand, "I'll help you up." Chloe got up. "Max, what do you have to say to Chloe?"

Max pretended he didn't hear. He was really good at that.

Miss Clark put her hands on Max's shoulders and slowly turned him around to face Chloe. "Max," she repeated. "You owe Chloe an apology."

Silence.

Chloe put her hands on her hips. "I'm waiting for my apology."

"Sorry," Max mumbled.

"Please look at her when you say it, and say it a little bit louder so she can hear you," said Miss Clark.

"Sorry!" Max said loudly.

"Thank you," said Miss Clark. She picked up Chloe's lunch box. "Here you go. I think your lunch box will be okay," she said. "Luckily, it's the soft kind, so you can just push it back the way it was."

"But it is brand-new," Chloe sniffled.

"And it's beautiful," said Miss Clark. "Pretty in pink, just like you. Why don't you go put it away, so we can get our morning started?"

Chloe twirled around twice, holding her lunch box high above her head, and then put it gently in her cubby.

"Boys and girls, please come to the rug," said Miss Clark. "I have some very exciting news to tell you."

"I can't wait to hear what it is," said Jessie.

"Me either!" I said.

When everyone was sitting quietly, Miss Clark said, "This morning Principal Pendergast told me that there is going to be a Second Grade Spelling Bee!"

"A Spelling Bee! Really?" said Jessie.

"Really," Miss Clark answered.

"I've always wanted to be in a Spelling Bee," I said, grinning.

"Well, I guess it's your lucky day!" said Miss Clark.

It sure is, I thought to myself, patting my lucky shark's tooth.

"Is the Spelling Bee just for our class?" asked Chloe.

"No, Fancypants," Max barked. "She just said it was the whole second grade."

"The whole second grade is a lot of kids," said Josh.

"Eighty children, to be exact," said Miss Clark.

"The winner is going to have to spell a lot of words!" said Jessie.

"That's right," said Miss Clark. "A *lot*."

"Does the winner get a prize?" asked Max.

"Yes," said Miss Clark. "The winner gets a twenty-five dollar gift certificate to the bookstore."

"Oh, I really want to win," said Jessie. "Last week when I was at the mall, I saw three new books I wanted in the bookstore window."

"Then you'll need to do a lot of studying," said Miss Clark. "It will take a lot of hard work, but I know you can do it."

I patted my pocket again. Jessie may have to study hard, but I didn't. I had my lucky shark's tooth.

CHAPTER 3

Ooey, Gooey Worms

When it was recess time, Josh, Jessie, and I ran outside to meet Robbie on the playground.

"Race you to the big tree," said Jessie. "Ready, set, go!"

The three of us took off running. Josh started out in the lead, but Jessie sprinted past him. Josh tried to catch up to her, but he couldn't. Jessie reached the tree first.

"You . . . are . . . so . . . fast . . . Jessie," Josh said, panting.

"She's the fastest kid in the whole school," I said.

"No I'm not," Jessie said, laughing.

"Well, you're really, really fast," I said. "I'm pretty sure you could beat most of the fifth graders."

Robbie came jogging up. "Hey, guys," he said.

"Hey, what's up?" we all said.

"You guys ready to go look for worms?"

"Yes!" said Josh, pumping his fist in the air. "The bigger, the better!"

"A big, fat, juicy worm is the best kind," Jessie said, grinning.

"Where do you think we should go look?" I asked Robbie.

"Let's go check out that mud puddle over near the slide. I think we might find a lot of worms in there."

We all ran over to the mud and got down on our hands and knees.

"I think we might have to dig around in the mud a little bit to find them," said Robbie. "Sometimes they like to hide."

We started digging through the mud. It was cool, and squishy, and gooey. "This is great mud for making mud pies!" I said, letting the mud ooze through my fingers.

"I love playing in the mud," said Josh. "It's so much fun!"

"Found any worms yet?" asked Robbie.

"Not yet!" I said.

"Me either," said Josh.

"I found one! I found one!" Jessie shouted.

Just then Chloe slid down the slide and came

running over to us. "What did you find, Jessie?" she asked excitedly. "Did you find a jewel?"

"A jewel?" Josh whispered to me. "Where does she think we're digging, ancient Egypt?"

I laughed.

"No! I didn't find a jewel. I found this," Jessie said, dangling the huge, slimy worm in Chloe's face.

"EEEWWW! EEEWWW! EEEWWW!" Chloe screamed and flapped her arms around

wildly in the air. "Get that thing away from me! Get it away!"

Jessie put the worm in the palm of her hand. "But it's so cute."

"Cute! Cute? It is not cute!" Chloe shouted. "It is DIS-GUS-TING!"

"No it's not," said Jessie, bringing the worm up close to her own face, as if she were about to kiss it.

"Yes it is," said Chloe. "It's dirty and disgusting, and it has germs. Lots and lots of germs!"

"So you don't want to hold it?" Jessie teased.

"No I don't! I'm going to play somewhere else!" said Chloe, and she turned around and marched off.

"Little worm, say bye-bye to Chloe," said Jessie.

"That girl is unbelievable," said Josh. "But at least now I know that if I want to get rid of her, all I have to do is show her a worm!"

I chuckled. "We'll have to remember that for April Fools' Day."

"Good idea," said Josh. "Maybe we could put a gummy worm in her sandwich. That would really freak her out!"

"I can picture it now," I said. "She'd be jumping around and screaming, 'Help! Help! I ate a worm. Call 911! Call 911!'"

"HA! HA! HA! HA! HA!" Josh and I laughed hysterically.

"Hey, guys, I got one!" Robbie yelled. "Come look!"

"Wow! That one is ginormous!" I said. "I think it might be bigger than Jessie's worm."

"Let me see," said Jessie. "I don't know. Mine might be bigger."

"Why don't you hold the two of them next to each other, so you can compare their size," Josh suggested.

"Good idea," said Robbie. "Jessie, you hold yours up right next to mine, so we can measure."

They held up their worms.

"It's close," I said. "But I think Robbie's worm is bigger."

Then I heard a familiar voice. "What are you babies doing?"

It was Max.

"I thought you were playing tag," said Josh.

"I was, but I got bored, so I came over here to see what you wimps were doing."

"We're looking for worms," said Josh.

"Did you find any?" asked Max.

"Yeah. I found one and Robbie found one," said Jessie.

"Can I see them?" said Max.

Robbie and Jessie held out their worms for Max to see. He grabbed the worms out of their hands.

"Hey, give those back! Those are ours," Jessie said.

"Not anymore," Max said, grinning. "Now they're mine." And he ran off with the worms.

"I can't believe he just did that," I said.

"He's such a bully," said Josh.

"I really wanted to bring my worm inside and show it to Miss Clark," said Jessie. "I think she would have thought it was cool."

"Hey," said Robbie. "Did Miss Clark tell your class about the Second Grade Spelling Bee?"

"Yeah, she told us about it this morning," I said.

"Isn't that so cool?" said Robbie excitedly. "I've always wanted to be in a Spelling Bee."

"I know," said Jessie. "Me too! I think it's going to be a lot of fun."

"It is going to be a lot of work," said Robbie. "Did you see how many words are on the list they gave us to study?"

"How many?" I asked.

"One hundred," said Jessie.

"One hundred?" said Josh. "No way!"

Jessie nodded her head. "Yep. One hundred words."

"That's a lot of words," said Josh. "I don't think I can learn that many."

"Of course you can," said Robbie. "You just need to work hard and study the words every night. Right, Freddy?"

"Well, I won't have to study too much," I said.

"Why not?" asked Jessie. "Do you have some kind of superpowers?"

"No, I don't have superpowers," I said, laughing. "But I do have my lucky shark's tooth."

"You can't just depend on that," said Robbie.

"Yes, I can," I said. "It always brings me good luck."

"What happens if you lose it?" Josh asked. "You know I have a lucky shark's tooth, too, and one time I lost mine. I couldn't find it for a week!"

"I don't have to worry about that. I never lose mine," I said, patting my pocket. "It's always right here."

CHAPTER 4

Mud Monster

When I got home from school, I went straight to the kitchen to get a snack.

"What happened to you?" my mom asked.

"What do you mean?" I said.

"Just look at you! You're covered in mud."

"Yeah," said Suzie. "You look like you went swimming in a mud puddle."

"Oh, that," I said, laughing. "My friends and I were looking for worms at recess today."

"Did you have to do that in the mud?" said my mom.

"That's the best place to find worms," I said, "especially after it rains."

"You guys must have been in that big puddle near the slide," said Suzie. "I stayed far away from it."

"That seems like a better idea," said my mom.

"I'm starving," I said. "Can I please have a snack?"

"Not until you change your clothes and wash your hands *really* well," said my mom. "Right now you look like a mud monster."

"Okeydokey!" I shouted as I ran out of the kitchen and dashed up the stairs. "I'll be right back!"

"And make sure you put those muddy clothes in the hamper, not on the floor," my mom called after me.

My mom was such a neat freak. Our toys always had to be put away. We weren't allowed to have food in our bedrooms, we had to make our beds every morning, and absolutely no pets allowed in the house!

I quickly changed my clothes and tossed the muddy ones into the dirty clothes hamper in the bathroom. Then I scrubbed my hands with soap. As the dirt washed off, it made a muddy river in the sink.

I dried my hands, and in my rush to get back to the kitchen, I slid down the banister instead of taking the stairs.

The only problem was I almost slid right into Suzie, who was just starting to walk up the stairs. I froze.

"Ooooooo, you are in so much trouble," said Suzie. "You know you're never supposed to slide down the banister."

"No one will know unless you tell them," I whispered. "And you wouldn't tell Mom and Dad, right?"

"What's it worth to you?" Suzie asked as she held up her pinkie for a pinkie swear.

"Really?" I said. "You won't keep this a secret?"

"I will if we make a deal," Suzie answered with a big grin on her face.

"Fine, fine," I said. "I'll make your bed tomorrow morning."

"Just tomorrow morning?" said Suzie. "You've got to be kidding."

"Well, how many mornings do you want me to make it?"

"Three," said Suzie, shoving three fingers in my face.

"I can count," I said. "I don't need your fingers in my face."

"So do we have a deal?" Suzie asked, holding up her pinkie one more time.

"Yes! We have a deal," I shouted, and we locked pinkies.

Just as we finished, my mom appeared. "Kids, what's going on in here? Is everything all right?"

I glared at Suzie. She made a deal. She'd better not tell my mom about what I just did, or the deal would be off.

"Yes, Mom, everything is okay," Suzie said.

"I heard Freddy shouting, so I thought I'd better come see if the two of you were okay."

"We're fine," I said. "Can I have my snack now please?"

"Sure, honey, come with me."

"I'll be right back down," Suzie said. "I just have to get something from my room."

My mom and I walked back into the kitchen. "Let me inspect those hands," said my mom. "I want to make sure you really did wash them."

I held out my hands for my mom to look at. First I held them palms up, and then I held them palms down. "See?" I said, smiling. "I washed the backs and the fronts."

"Nice job," said my mom. "Now what do you want to eat?"

"How about a cheese stick and some grapes?" I said.

"That sounds healthy," said my mom. "Good choice."

Suzie walked back into the kitchen. "Mom, did I just hear you say 'that sounds healthy'?"

"Yes, honey, you did."

"Since when does Freddy suggest a healthy snack?" said Suzie. "He has the biggest sweet tooth of anybody I've ever met!"

I crossed my arms and shouted, "I do not!"

"Yes you do!"

"Do not!"

"Do, too!"

"All right. Enough you two," said my mom. "There's no need to argue. Suzie, what would you like to eat?"

"I guess I'll have apple slices and peanut butter," she said.

"Another good choice," said my mom.

Suzie and I went to sit at the table while we waited for my mom to get our food.

"Here you go," said my mom, placing the snacks down in front of us.

I started to shove the cheese stick into my mouth.

"Whoa, slow down there, Freddy," said my mom. "You can't eat that whole thing at once."

"I'm just really hungry," I said with my mouth full.

"I can see that," said my mom, "But I don't want you to choke, and I don't want you to talk with your mouth full."

I picked up a grape, tipped my head back, opened my mouth, and tossed the grape in the

air. Instead of landing in my mouth, the grape hit Suzie in the face.

"Hey, watch it!" Suzie growled. "Don't throw grapes at me."

"I wasn't throwing grapes at you," I said. "I was trying to catch one in my mouth, but I missed."

"You missed by like a mile," said Suzie.

"Josh was trying to teach me how to catch grapes in my mouth during lunch today. He's really good at it."

"Well, you're not," said Suzie.

"Yes I am!" I shouted. "Watch!" I picked up another grape and tossed it in the air.

"Nice toss," Suzie teased.

This time the grape hit *me* in the eye.

"Bravo! Bravo!" Suzie yelled and clapped her hands. "That was amazing? Can you hit yourself in the eye again?"

"Be quiet!" I snapped. "You messed up my concentration when you yelled out 'nice toss'! I'm going to do it one more time, but you can't make any noise. I have to concentrate."

"I won't say a thing. My lips are sealed," said Suzie as she pretended to zip her lips closed.

This time before I threw the grape up into the air, I stuck my hand in my pocket and rubbed my lucky shark's tooth.

Then I tipped my head back, tossed the grape into the air, and it landed right in my mouth.

"Lucky throw," said Suzie. "That was just a lucky throw."

I just stared at her and smiled.

CHAPTER 5

Oh No!

The next morning, my alarm clock once again startled me out of a deep sleep. *RINNNGGG! RINNNGGG!*

And once again, I hit the snooze button. *Why does school have to start so early?* I thought to myself.

Just as I lay my head back down on my pillow, Suzie burst into the room and turned on the light.

"Hey! Turn that off!" I yelled. "I'm trying to sleep!"

"You need to get up right now!" Suzie barked.

"No I don't! I still have five more minutes," I said.

"Not this morning," Suzie said, grinning. "Remember, you have to make *two* beds this morning . . . mine and yours."

"UGH!" I groaned. "I forgot!"

"Well, I didn't forget," said Suzie. "A deal's a deal, so you'd better get your butt out of that bed."

"Okay, fine," I mumbled. "I'll get up in a minute. You can leave now."

But Suzie didn't leave. She kept standing there staring at me. I picked up a pair of jeans next to my bed and threw them at her. "Get out!" I shouted. "Now!"

Suzie started to back up toward the door. "If you don't make my bed this morning, then I'm going to tell Mom and Dad what you did yesterday."

"I'll make your bed. Now leave me alone!"

Suzie turned and left the room. I slowly

crawled out of bed and picked up the jeans I had thrown at her. I slid them on. I made sure I put my pants on first because I didn't want a repeat of what happened yesterday morning. That was embarrassing!

I finished getting dressed and tiptoed to the top of the stairs. I listened carefully for a minute. I could hear my mom, dad, and Suzie all down in the kitchen. The coast was clear. I slid down the banister and jogged into the kitchen. "Morning!" I said.

As soon as I came in, Suzie started pointing and laughing, "HA! HA! HA! HA! HA!"

What is she laughing at? I thought. I have pants on this morning. I know. I checked. "What's so funny?" I asked.

"Your . . . your . . . your . . . ," Suzie stammered.

"My what?"

"Your hair!"

I reached up to touch my hair. "What's wrong with my hair?"

"That's probably the worst bed head I've ever seen," Suzie said, laughing uncontrollably.

I looked over at my mom. "Did you forget to comb it this morning, honey?" she asked, trying not to laugh.

"Well . . . I . . . uh . . ."

"I think you'd better go back and comb your hair," said my mom.

"You might want to wet it with some water first," my dad suggested.

I dashed back up the stairs two at a time, ran into the bathroom, and looked in the mirror. My hair was sticking out all over the place. My head looked like a porcupine!

I wet my comb and dragged it through my hair, trying to tame the wild pieces. After a few minutes, I finally got most of it back in place.

I patted my head with my hands. "There. Much better."

I slid down the banister and ran back into the kitchen.

"You look like a whole new person," my mom said, smiling.

"While you were up there, did you take care of *everything*?" asked Suzie, raising her eyebrow.

Oh no, I thought to myself. I forgot to make her bed!

"Actually, there is one thing I forgot to do."

"Really, honey? What is it?" asked my mom.

"I . . . uh . . . I . . . uh . . . forgot to brush my teeth."

"Well, you'd better run back up and do that quickly," said my dad. "Or else you won't have time for breakfast."

Once again, I leaped up the stairs two at a time and dashed into Suzie's room. I grabbed her flowered sheets and yanked them up. Then I pulled up the pink blanket. Finally, I set the pillow in place.

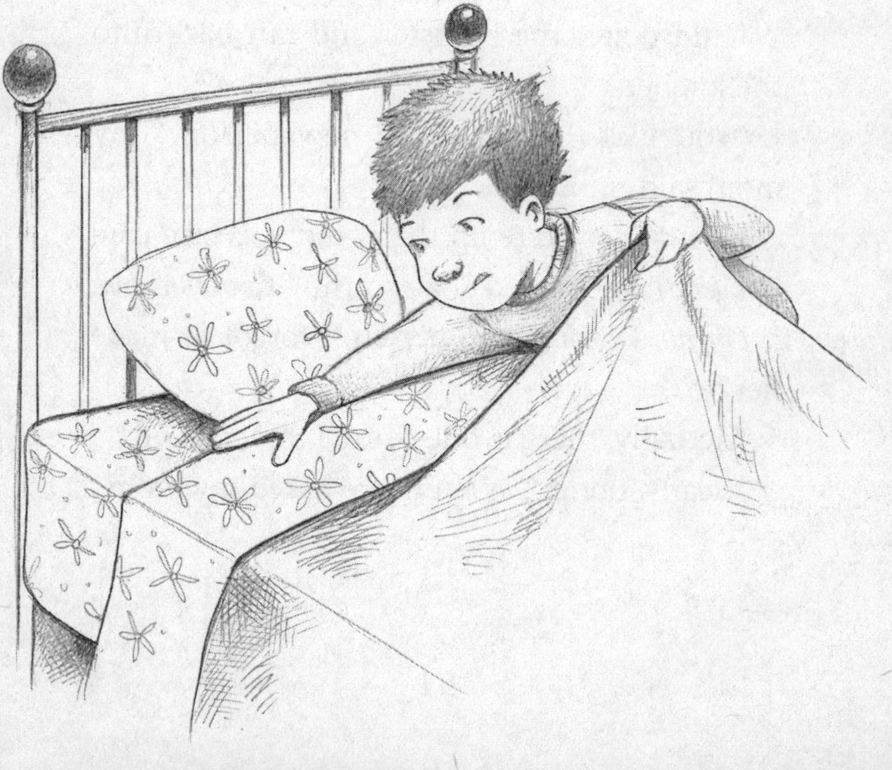

I turned to leave, and Suzie was standing in the doorway.

"What are you doing here?" I asked.

"I wanted to make sure you were making my bed the right way."

"What are you talking about?" I said. "There isn't a right way and a wrong way. It's just making a bed."

"Actually, you did do it wrong," said Suzie.

"Are you kidding me? What did I do wrong?"

"You didn't fluff the pillow."

"I didn't . . . what?"

"You didn't fluff the pillow," said Suzie. "You have to fluff up the pillow before you put it back on the bed."

I picked up the pillow, punched it a few times, and placed it back on the bed. "There. How's that, your highness?"

"Better," said Suzie. "Just don't forget to do that tomorrow."

I raced back downstairs. I couldn't slide down this time because Suzie was watching me.

"You might have to start getting up earlier, Freddy. You don't have much time left to eat," said my mom. "What do you want that's quick?"

"I'll just have a bagel and cream cheese this morning," I said. "I can always take that on the bus if I don't have time to finish it at home."

I had only taken two bites of my bagel when Suzie yelled, "The bus is here!"

"I guess you'll have to take your breakfast with you," said my mom.

I started to run out the door. "Freddy, come back!" she yelled. "You forgot your backpack!"

I grabbed my backpack off the counter. "Thanks, Mom! I'll see you after school," I called over my shoulder as I ran out the door and onto the bus.

I sat down next to Robbie and Josh. "Hey, guys, how's it going?"

Josh stretched his arms up and yawned. Robbie's eyelids looked droopy. "We're tired," they said.

"Why?" I asked.

"I did a lot of studying for the Spelling Bee last night," said Robbie. "My mom was testing me on the words."

"Me, too," said Josh. "My mom told me that I had to study the list of words every night if I wanted to do well."

"Freddy, what did your mom say?" asked Robbie.

"Nothing," I said.

"Nothing?" said Josh.

"I don't believe that," said Robbie. "I know your mom would help you study."

"Oh, she would if I asked," I said. "But I didn't ask. She doesn't even know about the Spelling Bee."

"Doesn't know about it?" said Robbie. "Why not?"

"Because I didn't tell her."

"But why not?" asked Josh.

"Because I don't need her help," I said.

"What do you mean you don't need her help?" said Robbie.

"I told you guys yesterday. I don't need to study. I have my lucky shark's tooth," I said, reaching into my pocket to give it a rub.

All of a sudden, I froze. My heart skipped a beat. "Oh no!" I shouted.

"What's wrong?" asked Josh and Robbie.

"My lucky shark's tooth . . . it's gone!"

CHAPTER 6

Lost!

"Maybe it's in your other pocket," Josh suggested. "I make that mistake sometimes."

"It's not in my other pocket. I know that for sure. I never switch pockets," I said anxiously.

"Why don't you just check?" said Robbie.

"It's not in there!" I shouted.

"Okay, okay," said Robbie. "You don't need to get angry. It was just a suggestion."

"Sorry, Robbie. I didn't mean to yell at you. I'm just freaking out right now," I said, feeling my panic rising.

"Why don't you stick your hand deep into both pockets," said Josh. "Just to be sure it's really not there."

I shoved my hand down into one pocket, and then the other. Nothing!

I shook my head. "This is terrible. No, it's worse than terrible. It's horrible!"

"You're like Alexander," said Robbie.

"Who?"

"*Alexander and the Terrible, Horrible, No Good, Very Bad Day.*"

"I love that book," said Josh.

"Me, too!" said Robbie. "My mom used to read it to me all the time before bed. It's one of my favorites."

"I love the part when he wakes up with gum in his hair," said Josh.

"How about when his mom forgets to pack dessert in his lunch box?" said Robbie. "You know that's happened to me before . . ."

"Hey! Hey!" I shouted. "Can you guys stop

talking about that book? I'm having a crisis here!"

"Oh yeah, sorry, Freddy," said Robbie. "Why don't you check under our seat here?"

"Good idea!" I said. "Maybe when I pulled the napkin out of my pocket to wipe the cream cheese off my nose, the shark's tooth accidentally fell out, too."

I bent down and looked under my bus seat.

"Do you see it?" asked Josh.

"I see a bubble gum wrapper, a broken pencil, and this cotton candy lip gloss," I said, holding up the gloss.

"What do you got there?" Max asked, pointing to the lip gloss.

"Nothing," I mumbled, hiding it behind my back.

"It looks like lip gloss to me," Max said, chuckling. "I bet you look adorable in that shade of pink."

"It's not mine!" I shouted.

"Let me see it," said Max, and he reached over the seat and grabbed it right out of my hands.

I tried to grab it back, but Max held it up high out of my reach.

"Hey, everybody, look at this," Max announced to the whole bus. "Freddy has cotton candy lip gloss."

My face turned bright red.

"It's not Freddy's. It's Max's," Josh said loudly.

Max narrowed his eyes at Josh. "No it's not! It's Freddy's!"

"If it belongs to Freddy, then why are you holding it?" asked Josh. "And it's pink. Isn't that your favorite color?"

Now Max turned bright red. He made a fist. "OOOOO, why you little . . ." he said and took a swing at Josh.

Josh grabbed Max's hand in midair before it landed on his face. "Keep your hands to yourself, you big bully."

Max tried to shake his hand loose, but Josh held on to it tightly. "Sit back down in your seat and leave Freddy alone."

Max glared at Josh, and then he slowly sat back down.

"Thanks, Josh," I whispered. "I can't believe you stopped Max's punch like that. What an awesome move."

"Yeah, it was just like out of the movies," said Robbie.

Josh laughed. "I was just protecting my friend."

"So you didn't see the shark tooth under the seat?" said Robbie.

I let out a big sigh. "Nope."

"Think hard," said Robbie. "When did you last have it?"

"Hmmmm, let's see." I hit my forehead with the palm of my hand. "Think, think, think. Oh, I know! I had it yesterday when I got home from school."

"How can you be so sure?" said Josh.

"Because I was tossing grapes into my mouth the way you were showing me at lunch yesterday."

"What does that have to do with your shark's tooth?" asked Josh. "Were you tossing the tooth into your mouth, too?"

"No!" I laughed. "I was trying to toss the grapes into my mouth, but I kept missing. Then I rubbed my lucky shark's tooth, and when I tossed again, the grape landed right in my mouth."

"It really does bring you good luck," said Robbie.

"I know! That's why I've got to find it!"

"Well, it shouldn't be too hard to find," said Josh. "It's got to be in your house somewhere."

"Not necessarily," I said.

"What do you mean?" said Robbie. "You said you had it at home yesterday, so you know you didn't lose it at school."

"But I wasn't just in the house," I said.

"Where else did you go?" asked Josh.

"I went outside to play in the backyard for a while. Then I went down the street to visit Mrs. Golden and her dog Baxter."

"Oh, I see what you mean," said Robbie. "It really could be anywhere."

"Thanks a lot," I said. "That doesn't make me feel better. It makes me feel worse."

"Stop worrying so much," said Robbie. "It will turn up. Whenever I lose something, I always find it eventually."

"But I can't wait for it to turn up," I said.

"Why not?" said Josh.

"Because the Spelling Bee is in three days!" I cried.

"So?" said Robbie.

"So, I'm not going to do well without my lucky shark's tooth!"

"Yes you will," said Josh.

"No I won't! I'm going to fail and totally embarrass myself."

"I know how you can do well even without your lucky shark's tooth," said Robbie.

I turned to look right at him. "Oh really. How? I'm not a genius like you."

"By studying," said Robbie. "If you study hard, you'll do really well even without your lucky shark's tooth."

"You really think so?"

"I know so," said Robbie.

"Robbie's right," said Josh. "That's why the two of us were studying so hard last night. Whenever I'm surfing, my dad always says, 'practice makes perfect.'"

"Hey, I have an idea," said Robbie. "Why don't Josh and I come over after school every day this week and help you study?"

"You guys would do that for me?" I said.

"Of course!" said Robbie.

"That's what friends are for," said Josh.

CHAPTER 7

Practice Makes Perfect

Every day after school, Robbie and Josh came over to my house to help me study. We worked really hard. One hundred words is a lot to learn!

"I can't believe the Spelling Bee is tomorrow!" said Josh on Thursday afternoon.

"I think we're ready," said Robbie.

"I don't think I'm going to do very well," I mumbled.

"Why not?" said Josh.

"Because I still haven't found my lucky shark's tooth."

"But you don't need your lucky shark's tooth for good luck," said Robbie.

"Yes I do!" I said. "I'm going to fail without it!"

"No you won't," said Robbie. "You know how to spell the words because you studied really hard."

"You don't need that good-luck charm," said Josh. "You just have to believe in yourself. You have to think, 'I can do this!'"

I sighed and put my head in my hands. "I guess I don't really have a choice."

"And remember the little tricks I taught you," said Robbie. "Like 'i' before 'e' except after 'c.'"

"Like in the word 'field' the 'i' comes before the 'e' because there is no 'c,' said Josh. "But in the word 'receive,' the 'e' comes before the 'i' because there is a 'c' in front of it."

4:15
DICTIONARY

"Or if a word ends in an 'e,' said Robbie, "you drop the 'e' before adding 'ing.' So how would you spell the word 'coming'?"

I thought for a minute. "C-O-M-I-N-G."

"Right!" said Robbie, patting me on the back.

"You spelled that perfectly," said Josh, "and you didn't need your lucky shark's tooth."

"There is another problem," I said.

"What's that?" asked Josh.

"My lucky shark's tooth doesn't just bring me luck. Rubbing it also helps me calm down, and I know I'm going to be really nervous up there on that stage."

"Everybody is going to be nervous," said Josh.

"But I get *really* nervous." I said, wringing my hands. "Sometimes my stomach is flipping and flopping so much that I feel like I'm going to throw up."

"Then definitely don't stand next to me!" Josh laughed.

"Or me!" said Robbie.

"Thanks a lot, guys," I said.

"We're just kidding," they both said.

"You know there are lots of things you can do to try to calm yourself down," said Robbie.

"Really? Like what?"

"If I get really nervous, I usually just breathe in and out very slowly. I take nice, deep breaths like this," said Robbie, breathing in and out, in and out. "Try it."

I took a couple of quick, short breaths.

"Not like that," Robbie said, laughing. "That's way too fast. You need to breathe much, much slower. You can even count in your head. Breathe in for three counts and out for three counts. Like this." Robbie demonstrated. "Now it's your turn."

I tried again. This time I counted in my head like Robbie told me to.

"You got it! That was perfect!" said Robbie.

"Do you want to know what I do?" asked Josh.

"Sure!" I said.

"I think of a song I really like, and I hum it quietly to myself. Then I'm thinking about the song and not about being nervous."

"That sounds like a good idea, too," I said.

"Remember that funny song Miss Clark was teaching us the other day about the kid who was going to eat some worms?"

"Yeah! I loved that song!" I said.

"That would be a good one to hum," said Josh. "It's just so funny."

I started humming it quietly to myself. Robbie and Josh joined in. Then we all burst out laughing hysterically.

"Thank, guys. You're the best," I said, giving Robbie and Josh each a high five.

"I'm tired of being inside," Josh moaned.

"Me, too," said Robbie.

"I have an idea," said Josh. "Let's go outside and throw the baseball around. We can practice spelling the words as we throw the ball back and forth to each other."

"Great idea!" I said. "I'm sick of sitting in this room."

We grabbed our baseball gloves and a ball and headed outside.

We stood in a triangle and threw the ball to each other as we spelled words out loud, one letter for each throw.

"B-E-C-A-U-S-E."

"S-P-E-C-I-A-L."

"H-A-V-I-N-G."

All of a sudden, Mrs. Golden's dog, Baxter,

came bounding up and knocked me to the ground. The baseball rolled out of my glove. Baxter picked it up in his mouth and started running in circles with it.

I chased him around the yard shouting, "Come here, boy! Give that back!"

Robbie and Josh also joined the chase. "Here, boy! Here, boy!" they called, but Baxter didn't stop running.

"He is fast!" Josh said, panting.

"How are we going to catch him?" said Robbie. "We need that ball back, but he doesn't want to give it up."

"I know what I'll do," I said. I took a flying leap, landed on Baxter's back, and tackled him to the ground. "Gotcha!" I yelled.

Baxter dropped the ball and covered my face with wet, slobbery dog kisses. I laughed. "Thanks, boy. Thanks for the kisses."

Josh ran to pick up the ball. "EEEWWW! This is disgusting!" he said, holding the ball carefully between two fingers. "It's covered in slimy dog saliva."

"Roll it around in the grass to wipe it off," Robbie suggested.

I slowly stood up and wiped my face with my sleeve. "Where's your mama, Baxter?" I said. "Where's Mrs. Golden?"

"I'm right here! I'm right here!" Mrs. Golden called as she came jogging up the street. "I'm so sorry about that, boys," she said. "He took off before I could get his leash on."

"No problem," I said. "I think Baxter wanted to play baseball."

Mrs. Golden walked over to Baxter. "Come over here, you naughty boy. Let me get your leash on." She hooked the leash onto his collar. "There. Now you can't take off again without me."

"Where are you off to?" I asked Mrs. Golden.

"I was actually coming over to see you, Freddy. I found something lying in the grass in my front yard the other day, and I was wondering if it belonged to you."

"Oh really?"

Mrs. Golden reached into her pocket and pulled something out. She slowly opened up her hand to show me what it was. I couldn't believe my eyes.

Was it? Could it really be? My lucky shark's tooth!

CHAPTER 8

The Spelling Bee

It was finally Friday. "Is everybody ready for the Spelling Bee?" asked Miss Clark.

I stuck my hand in my pocket and rubbed my lucky shark's tooth. *I am,* I thought to myself.

I leaned over to Josh and whispered, "I'm so glad I found my shark's tooth just in time!"

"But you don't really need it," said Josh.

"Yes I do!"

"Not really," said Josh. "You know all of the words because you studied really hard all week."

"This is how it's going to work," said Miss Clark. "This morning before recess, all of the second-grade teachers are going to give their students a spelling test of fifty words. The ten children who get the highest score will then compete against each other to see who is the second grade spelling champion."

My stomach flip-flopped. Fifty words!

Josh looked over at me. "Are you okay, Freddy? You look a little pale."

"I don't know."

"You can do this," said Josh. "Just breathe."

Miss Clark passed out the paper, and we all took the test. As we were passing them in, Josh whispered, "So, Freddy, how do you think you did?"

"I think I did okay," I said, smiling. "Thanks to you and Robbie."

After recess Miss Clark said, "Well, it's time to go to the gym and join the other second-grade classes. When we get there, Mr. Pendergast will tell you who the finalists are."

We all followed Miss Clark into the gym. It was buzzing with excitement. I saw Robbie out of the corner of my eye and waved.

He gave me two thumbs up and mouthed, "Good luck!"

Principal Pendergast, stepped up to the microphone. "Welcome, everybody," he said. "I hope you are as excited about this Spelling Bee as I am."

Chloe stood up and waved her hands in the air. "Yoo-hoo! Mr. Pendergast! I just want you

to know I am super excited. I even wore this brand-new dress today just for the occasion. Isn't it beautiful?"

"It's lovely, dear," said Mr. Pendergast. "Now please sit down."

Chloe started to twirl around, but Miss Clark grabbed her hand and gently pulled her back into her seat.

Mr. Pendergast continued, "Right before recess, you all took a test of fifty words that were on your list. I am very proud of all of you, but today only the ten children who got the best scores will compete for the title of Second Grade Spelling Champion."

"That's going to be me!" Max yelled out.

"Really? How does *he* know that?" Josh whispered to me.

I shrugged my shoulders.

"If everyone is quiet, then I will read the names of the ten finalists. When you hear your name, please come up on the stage."

I rubbed my lucky shark's tooth.

"Shanvi, Carlos, Robbie, James, Chloe, Li-Jing, Max, Fatima, Jessie, and . . ."

My heart skipped a beat.

"Freddy."

Josh shook me. "Dude! That's awesome! He said your name. You're one of the finalists."

"I think I'm going to throw up," I said. "I can't go up there in front of all these people."

"Yes you can. Remember what I told you to do yesterday. If you get really nervous, just hum a song quietly in your head."

Josh gave me a little push. "Now get up there."

I slowly walked up the steps to the stage. My legs were so wobbly. They felt like Jell-O.

Max and Chloe were pushing and shoving each other. "This is my spot," Chloe whined.

"No, I was here first!" Max shouted.

"But my name was called before yours," Chloe cried.

"So what?" barked Max. "Get out of my way."

Mr. Pendergast came rushing over. "If the two of you don't stop arguing right now, then you will both be out of the competition. Understand?"

Max glared at Chloe. Chloe glared at Max.

"Do you understand?"

They both nodded their heads.

"Okay, I think we are ready to begin," said Mr. Pendergast. "I will tell you a word, and you have to spell it out loud for us. If you spell it correctly, then you will move on to the next

round. If you don't spell it correctly, then you will sit down."

After ten rounds, there were four kids left, Jessie, Max, Shanvi, and me! I had made it through ten rounds!

The competition continued and after fourteen rounds, there were only two kids left . . . Max Sellars, and me! I couldn't believe it. I never win anything, but here I was so close to winning the whole thing.

"You know you're not going to win," Max whispered in my ear.

"How do you know?" I whispered back.

"Because no one beats me. I'm the best at everything."

I shifted slightly away, so I didn't have to feel his hot, stinky breath on my neck.

I looked out into the audience searching for Josh and Robbie. Josh looked up at me and mouthed, "You got this!"

Then I saw Robbie. He held up three fingers

and touched his lips to remind me to breathe slowly to a count of three.

It was Max's turn. "Okay, Max," said Mr. Pendergast. "Are you ready for your next word?"

"Of course," Max said. "Give it to me."

"Your word is 'special.'" Please spell the word 'special.'"

"Oh, that one's easy," said Max with a big grin on his face. "S-P-E-C-I-L. Special."

"No, I am sorry. That is incorrect," said Mr. Pendergast.

Max's mouth dropped open and he stamped his foot. "No it's not!" he shouted. "I know I spelled it right."

"Now it's Freddy's turn to spell that word," said Mr. Pendergast. "If he spells it right, then he will be the winner."

I stuck my hand in my pocket and rubbed my lucky shark's tooth. *I know this one,* I thought to myself. We just studied it yesterday.

I slowly took a deep breath, in for three counts and out for three counts. Then I stepped up to the microphone and said, "S-P-E-C-I-A-L, special."

"That is correct!" said Mr. Pendergast. "Congratulations, Freddy. You are the Second Grade Spelling Champion!" and he handed me a big trophy and the gift certificate to the bookstore.

Josh and Robbie jumped out of their seats. "Woo-hoo!" they shouted. "You did it! You

won!" Then they started chanting, "Freddy! Freddy! Freddy!"

A huge smile spread across my face. *I am the luckiest person,* I thought to myself. I have the best friends ever!

Freddy's Fun Pages

10 SUPER FUN WAYS TO STUDY YOUR SPELLING WORDS!

Freddy has come up with some creative ways to study his weekly spelling words.

Which ones would you like to try? Remember to ask your parents for help (and permission)!

1. Pipe cleaner words: Bend and fold pipe cleaners to make letters and words.

2. Salt/sand/flour tray: Pour some salt, sand, or flour onto a tray and spell words using your finger. You can even do this with pudding and lick your fingers when you're done!

3. Q-tip writing: With Q-tips, paint lines of dots until you have letters and words.

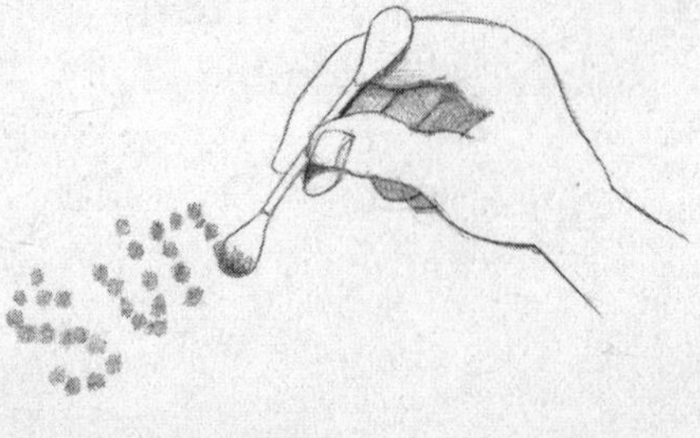

4. Hidden Words: Write words on a white piece of paper with a white crayon. Then paint over the words with watercolors and watch them magically appear!

5. Flashlight Words: Turn out the lights and write using only the light from your flashlight.

6. Shower Spelling: Spray shaving cream on your shower door and write with your finger.

7. Cereal Words: Use circle-shaped cereal like Cheerios to make letters in your bowl.

8. Play-Doh Words: Roll Play-Doh into thin strips to make letter shapes.

9. Finger Paint: Use a different color for each letter to make rainbow words!

10. Body Words: Trace your spelling words on someone's back or on your own palm!

CATCH A LEPRECHAUN! HIDDEN WORDS

Many people think it's good luck to catch a leprechaun because then he has to give you his pot of gold. How many words can you spell using the letters in the word LEPRECHAUN? (Freddy found the word NAP!) (Remember to only use each letter once—but you have two "e's"!)

LEPRECHAUN

____

____

____

____

____

GOOD-LUCK SYMBOLS

Can you use the clues to figure out each of these good-luck symbols? Write your answer on the line.

1. A plant that grows in Ireland ____________

____

2. Something a horse wears ______________

____

3. A coin made of copper ________________

____

4. A red insect with black spots __________

____

5. Something that pandas like to eat _______

____

6. A turkey part you save at Thanksgiving

____

7. A type of fish you might keep as a pet

____

8. Part of a rabbit's body ________________

____

9. Something some Native Americans hang next to their beds ______________________________

____

10. Something you might see in the sky at night ______________________________

Answers:

1. four-leaf clover
2. horseshoe
3. penny
4. ladybug
5. bamboo
6. wishbone
7. goldfish
8. rabbit's foot
9. dreamcatcher
10. star (shooting star, falling star)

Get Ready for
Ready, Freddy!
Ready, Set, Snow!
Firehouse Fun!
The Perfect Present
The Penguin Problem
Apple Orchard Race
Going Batty
Science Fair Flop
A Very Crazy Christmas
Shark Attack!
Save the Earth!
The Giant Swing
The Reading Race
2nd Grade
Second Grade Rules!
Snow Day Dare
by ABBY KLEIN
Illustrated by JOHN McKINLEY
SCHOLASTIC